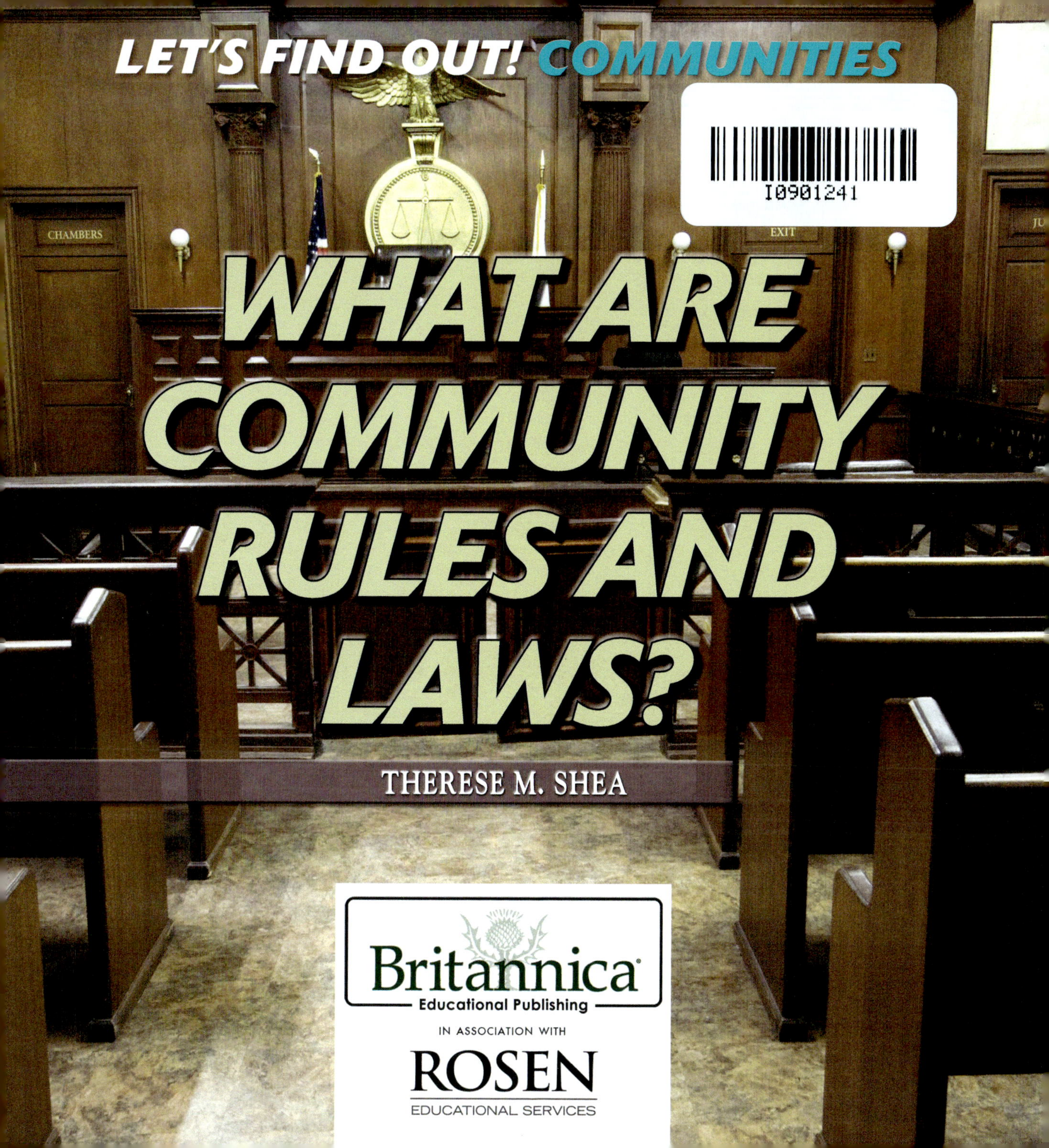

LET'S FIND OUT! COMMUNITIES

WHAT ARE COMMUNITY RULES AND LAWS?

THERESE M. SHEA

Britannica Educational Publishing
IN ASSOCIATION WITH
ROSEN
EDUCATIONAL SERVICES

Published in 2018 by Britannica Educational Publishing (a trademark of Encyclopædia Britannica, Inc.) in association with The Rosen Publishing Group, Inc.
29 East 21st Street, New York, NY 10010

Distributed exclusively by Rosen Publishing.
To see additional Britannica Educational Publishing titles, go to rosenpublishing.com.

First Edition

Britannica Educational Publishing
J.E. Luebering: Executive Director, Core Editorial
Mary Rose McCudden: Editor, Britannica Student Encyclopedia

Rosen Publishing
Bernadette Davis: Editor
Nelson Sá: Art Director
Matt Cauli: Designer
Ellina Litmanovich: Book Layout
Cindy Reiman: Photography Manager
Karen Huang: Photo Researcher

Library of Congress Cataloging-in-Publication Data

Names: Shea, Therese, author.
Title: What are community rules and laws? / Therese M. Shea.
Description: First edition. | New York : Britannica Educational Publishing, 2018. | Series: Let's find out! Communities | Includes bibliographical references and index.
Identifiers: LCCN 2016056211 | ISBN 9781680487213 (pbk. book : alk. paper) | ISBN 9781680487220 (6 pack : alk. paper) | ISBN 9781680487237 (library bound book : alk. paper)
Subjects: LCSH: Law—Juvenile literature. | Law—United States—Juvenile literature.
Classification: LCC K240 .S52 2017 | DDC 340—dc23
LC record available at https://lccn.loc.gov/2016056211

Manufactured in the United States of America

Photo credits: Cover, pp. 1, 17, 24, interior pages (background) bikeriderlondon/Shutterstock.com; p. 4 Blend Images/Shutterstock.com; p. 5 Monkey Business Images/Shutterstock.com; p. 6 klohka/iStock/Thinkstock; p. 7 Owen Franken/Corbis Documentary/Getty Images; p. 8 Denis Belitsky/Shutterstock.com; p. 9 George Doyle/Stockbyte/Thinkstock; p. 10 Lisa S./Shutterstock.com; p. 11 wavebreakmedia/Shutterstock.com; p. 12 Print Collector/Hulton Archive/Getty Images; p. 13 Private Collection/The Stapleton Collection/Bridgeman Images; p. 14 Photos.com/Thinkstock; pp. 15, 21 © iStockphoto.com/RichLegg; p. 16 Mark Wilson/Getty Images; p. 18 National Archives, Washington, DC; p. 19 Ognjen1234/Shutterstock.com; p. 20 Mat Hayward/Getty Images; p. 22 Comstock/Stockbyte/Getty Images; p. 23 Linda Patterson/Getty Images; p. 25 B Christopher/Alamy Stock Photo; p. 26 Gary Corbett/age footstock/Superstock; pp. 27, 29 Bloomberg/Getty Images; p. 28 Gino Santa Maria/Shutterstock.com.

Contents

WHO NEEDS RULES?

A rule is a guideline for how to behave. Rules are everywhere: at home, at school, and wherever else people interact with each other. At home, parents set rules that teach children how to behave, such as no hitting your brother or sister. Rules at school can include raising your hand to talk and sitting in your seat until the teacher tells you to get up. Though some rules can seem unnecessary at times, they are important. If everyone talked

Rules help manage the work of a household and keep families safe.

The teachers and the principal set many of the rules of a school.

or moved around the class whenever they wanted, it would be hard for students to pay attention to the teacher and to learn.

Rules are not just for young people at home and in school. Everyone needs rules. That is why rules are a part of every kind of community. All governments have a set of official rules called laws that everyone must obey.

Think About It

Think of another rule in school and the reasons why that rule is important.

Communities and Rules

A community is a group of people with common interests. People usually belong to more than one community. For instance, a neighborhood is one kind of community and a school is another kind. There are even online communities where people talk or play games. All of these communities need rules so that the communities continue to work well and support people's interests and goals.

This school bus's stop sign tells other drivers to stop and be aware of crossing children.

This city council is making decisions for the community.

Communities in which people live, from small villages to large countries, have governments that make rules requiring or prohibiting certain actions. These rules are called laws. Laws keep order and protect people.

COMPARE AND CONTRAST

Think of two communities you are a part of. Do they have the same kinds of rules or different rules? Why are they the same or different?

Rules and Responsibility

Different kinds of communities have different laws that make life better for people in those places. For example, some cities have zoning laws that say noisy or smelly factories cannot be built in certain zones, or areas, where people live. There may be laws and rules in special parts of communities, too. For example, in order to keep people safe after dark, visitors often need to leave city or state parks by sunset.

People have a responsibility to the other members of their community to

Rules for factories and businesses protect communities from pollution.

COMPARE AND CONTRAST

What special laws might a big city need that a small town would not? Why?

This police officer is writing someone a ticket for breaking a traffic law.

follow laws that keep the community working well. Also, there are consequences for not following laws. Many communities have organizations for enforcing laws and keeping order. One of these organizations is a police force.

Natural and Positive Laws

Law that is based on a common code of conduct among all humans is called natural law. Stealing and killing are both forbidden by natural law. These natural laws are translated into community laws throughout the world.

Law that is based on rules created by rulers

Most societies are against stealing, so that is a natural law that is usually a positive law as well.

Judges often rule on the fact that a law has been broken and decide what punishment fits the crime.

or lawmakers is called positive law. Speed limits on roads are positive laws. Most natural laws have become adopted as positive laws.

Lawmaking bodies of government called legislatures make laws. The United States, Canada, and the United Kingdom, as well as some other countries, also get laws from the decisions of judges.

Think About It

Think of another law that was probably a natural law. Why do you think it was a natural law before it became a positive law?

History of Law

Written laws emerged as soon as humans started writing. One of the best known of the early codes, or collections of written laws, is that of Hammurabi. He was a king of Babylon who lived almost three thousand years ago. Probably the most famous of the ancient codes, however, is found in the first five books of the Bible. The heart of this code is the Ten Commandments. The commandments are a

This carved stone column displays Hammurabi on his throne passing down his famous laws.

An illustration shows citizens of ancient Greece discussing an important issue.

basic summary of moral laws that tell Christians how to behave.

All other societies in the ancient world created sets of laws. In the democracy of ancient Athens in Greece, the citizens agreed on the laws that would govern them. Modern democracies, including the United States and Canada, borrow from this practice.

Vocabulary

A **democracy** is a government in which the citizens vote in order to have a say in how the government is run.

Systems of Law

Most modern countries follow one of two systems of law: common or civil. Common law developed in England hundreds of years ago. Judges make decisions about cases based on decisions in earlier cases. British settlers brought common law with them to the North American colonies of England that became the United States.

In Europe and Latin America, many countries base their laws on the civil code. French emperor Napoleon I introduced this wide-reaching system of laws in 1804. It was meant to break free from

Emperor Napoleon I introduced a set of laws called the civil code to the French in 1804.

This judge is presiding over a case. It is her job to make sure it is a fair case.

past laws that were unfair to certain groups of people. Judges relying on the Napoleonic civil code use the laws instead of past judgments to make decisions.

The United States mostly follows common law, except for the state of Louisiana, which has a civil code. In Canada, only the province of Quebec practices civil law.

Compare and Contrast

What do you think are the advantages and disadvantages of common law and civil law?

This photograph shows a meeting of Congress in Washington, DC.

The United States uses statute law in addition to common law. A statute law is made by a legislature. In the United States, Congress passes federal laws in Washington, DC. Each state also has its own legislature that makes statute laws strictly for that state. Statute laws are made in local lawmaking bodies in smaller communities as well, such as in city councils and town councils.

Judges must be familiar with both statutory law and common law.

Statute laws developed because common law does not apply in all cases. Sometimes statute laws deal with situations that are so new that a judge cannot look at decisions from earlier cases. Statute laws can also be a way to make the decisions from common law official. Statute laws include regulations about education, taxes, and protecting the environment.

Think About It

Do you think laws about the internet are common or statute laws? Why?

Federal and State Laws

The United States **Constitution** is the most basic law of the United States. It describes the branches of the government and their separate powers. The Constitution also gives the federal, or national, government the power to make certain laws.

Vocabulary

A **constitution** is a set of laws by which a country or state is governed.

Federal laws apply to everyone in the whole country, even the smallest community. These laws

The United States Constitution was written in 1787 and approved by the states in 1788.

include regulations about immigration, federal crimes (such as not paying your taxes), and many other things.

The Constitution makes sure that each state has the power to make laws that must be obeyed within that state. Laws may be different from state to state. State laws deal with crime, businesses, family law, and even how long a student must attend school.

Other countries have similar systems of law. In Canada, there are laws for the provinces and territories as well as federal laws.

Canada's federal legislature, the Parliament, meets in Ottawa, Ontario.

Criminal Law

There are two main branches of law: criminal and civil. Criminal law deals with crime, which occurs when a person breaks a law. Crimes are harmful to communities. They include such acts as murder, robbery, and assault. They also include offenses that may seem harmless, such as driving through a stop sign, but that could result in injury or death. The government usually puts people accused of breaking laws on trial in a court. If the court finds the accused—called the defendant—guilty, he or she is punished.

Police solve crimes and try to keep people safe.

People who are accused of crimes are usually put on trial in a court.

Punishments depend on the seriousness of the crime. Less serious crimes such as shoplifting may be punished with a fine or community service. More serious crimes result in a prison term or even death.

In the United States, the government may be the federal, state, or local authority, depending on the law that has been broken.

Think About It

Why are crimes such as murder and robbery considered harmful to communities as a whole rather than just to the victim?

Civil Law

Civil law deals with disagreements between individuals. A person or group, also called a party, files a lawsuit in a civil court if they think another party has treated them unfairly. The party who files the suit is called the plaintiff. Usually the plaintiff wants money or a change in conduct from the opponent, called the defendant.

If the court agrees with the plaintiff, it will issue either an injunction or money damages against the defendant. An injunction is an order that the defendant must take

Defendants usually sit on the left side of a courtroom, but that is not always the case.

Compare and Contrast

How are criminal and civil cases similar? How are they different?

some action. For example, the defendant might have to deliver goods that were promised to the plaintiff in a contract. Divorce proceedings, claims of property damage, and arguments between landlords and tenants are all examples of civil cases.

These drivers may file a property damage claim in a civil court.

Courts, Judges, and Lawyers

Both civil and criminal cases are held in courts. The official in charge of each court is a judge. He or she hears the different sides of each case and makes decisions about the law. Judges often oversee a **jury**.

There are several different levels of courts within the United States. For example, breaking a state law requires a person to appear in a state court. If a defendant loses a case, he or she may challenge, or appeal, the decision in a

Both civil court and criminal court cases may have juries.

Law schools provide a general legal education for students who want to become attorneys.

higher court. Eventually a case may reach the Supreme Court, the highest court in the country.

The legal system is very complex. People who go to school to study the law are called lawyers or attorneys. They are used by both sides in court cases to make the arguments for and against the defendants.

Vocabulary

A **jury** is a group of regular citizens that are chosen to listen to both sides of a case and make decisions about the case.

Do Laws Change?

Our communities change all the time. Laws, too, are added or changed to address new problems. Consider how much technology has transformed the world. In many US states and all Canadian provinces, there are now laws against holding a cell phone while driving. These laws are meant to protect people from distracted driving.

Posted signs may remind people of newer laws in a certain area.

Justices of the Supreme Court of the United States change laws with some of their rulings.

People also demand that laws change to correct injustices. An amendment to the US Constitution finally gave women the right to vote in 1920. In 1990 the Americans with Disabilities Act guaranteed that people with physical or mental disabilities would have equal opportunities in their jobs, in schools, and in public places.

Think About It

Is there a rule that you think should be changed or a rule that should be added in your community? If so, what is it?

Changes to law do not always happen peacefully. Sometimes people protest to force change. They may disrupt daily activity so others pay attention and join their cause.

Living with Laws

People do not always agree on what should be illegal. Some people think there are too many laws and that the government should not be so involved in people's lives. For example, some people think there should be fewer laws about drugs. Others disagree with communities that outlaw foods that are bad for people's health. On the other hand, many citizens think more laws will keep

People often meet in public places to protest laws they don't like.

People of all ages and backgrounds are protected by the laws of their community.

communities safer and healthier.

People need to be active and informed about their community's laws. They should keep up to date about existing laws and about possible future laws that the government is considering. Everyone in a community can have a say about the laws in that community. They can write or email their government representative and state their opinion about how laws can help or hurt the lives of everyone in the community.

Think About It

Do you think laws limit freedoms or protect them? Give examples supporting your opinion.

GLOSSARY

amendment A change in wording or meaning especially in a law, bill, or motion.

assault An unlawful attempt or act of harm toward a person.

circumstance A condition at a certain time or place.

civil code A set of rules that define the law without relying on past judgements.

complex Having many parts, details, or ideas that can be hard to understand.

consequence A result or effect.

contract A legally binding agreement between two or more parties.

disrupt To throw into disorder.

distracted Drawing the attention or mind to something else.

enforcing Carrying out or bringing about, sometimes by force.

immigration The act of going to another country in order to live there.

legislature An organized body of persons having the authority to make laws.

moral Having to do with the judgment of right or wrong in human behavior.

prohibiting Not allowing.

province A large division of a country having its own government.

regulation A rule or order telling how something is to be done.

representative A person who represents, or acts for another, especially in government.

responsibility A duty or requirement.

summary A short statement of main points.

technology The use of science in solving problems.

For More Information

Books

Canfield, Michael. *America's Oddest Laws*. New York, NY: Gareth Stevens Publishing, 2016.

Keegan, Anna. *The United States Constitution and the Bill of Rights: The Law of the Land.* New York, NY: PowerKids Press, 2016.

Mara, Wil. *Law and Order.* Ann Arbor, MI: Cherry Lake Publishing, 2017.

Prentzas, G. S. *The Law and Your Family: Your Legal Rights.* New York, NY: Rosen Publishing, 2015.

Shea, Therese. *20 Fun Facts About the U.S. Constitution.* New York, NY: Gareth Stevens Publishing, 2014.

Slade, Suzanne. *A Bill's Journey into Law.* Mankato, MN: Picture Window Books, 2012.

Websites

Because of the changing nature of internet links, Rosen Publishing has developed an online list of websites related to the subject of this book. This site is updated regularly. Please use this link to access the list:

http://www.rosenlinks.com/LFO/rules

INDEX